W9-BXL-583

In Our Neighborhood

Meet a Librarian!

by AnnMarie Anderson

Illustrations by Lisa Hunt

Bookmobile
Fountaindale Public Library
Bolingbrook, IL
(630) 759-2102

Children's Press®
An imprint of Scholastic Inc.

■SCHOLASTIC

Special thanks to our content consultants:

Mollie Surprenant
Children's Librarian
Rockport Public Library
Rockport, MA

Katherine Schwinden
School Librarian

Cathy Nuding
Youth Services Supervisor
East Fishkill Community Library
Hopewell Junction, NY

Library of Congress Cataloging-in-Publication Data

Names: Anderson, AnnMarie, author. | Hunt, Lisa, 1973– illustrator.

Title: In our neighborhood. Meet a librarian!/by AnnMarie Anderson; [illustrations by Lisa Hunt].

Other titles: Meet a librarian!

Description: New York: Children's Press, an imprint of Scholastic Inc., 2021. | Series: In our neighborhood | Includes index. | Audience: Ages 5–7. | Audience: Grades K–1. | Summary: "Two children learn the importance of librarians in their neighborhood"— Provided by publisher.

Identifiers: LCCN 2020031732 | ISBN 9780531136812 (library binding) | ISBN 9780531136874 (paperback)

Subjects: LCSH: Librarians— Juvenile literature. | Public libraries—Juvenile literature.

Classification: LCC Z682 .A57 2021 | DDC 020.92—dc23

LC record available at https://lccn.loc.gov/2020031732

Produced by Spooky Cheetah Press
Prototype design by Maria Bergós/Book & Look
Page design by Kathleen Petelinsek/The Design Lab

Printed in North Mankato, MN, USA 113

1 2 3 4 5 6 7 8 9 10 R 30 29 28 27 26 25 24 23 22 21

Scholastic Inc., 557 Broadway, New York, NY 10012.

Photos ©: 9: Independent Picture Service/Universal Images Group/Getty Images; 11: parkerphotography/Alamy Images; 15: Steve Skjold/Alamy Images; 16 left: Andersen Ross Photography Inc/Getty Images; 16 right: CWSteve Vidler/Alamy Images; 17 left: John Birdsall/Alamy Images; 17 right: Erik Isakson/Getty Images; 21: kali9/Getty Images; 22: SW Productions/Getty Images; 31 bottom left: TomBham/Alamy Images; 31 bottom right: Tyler Olson/Dreamstime.

All other photos © Shutterstock.

Table of Contents

OUR NEIGHBORHOOD

Hi! I'm Emma. This is my best friend, Theo. Welcome to our neighborhood!

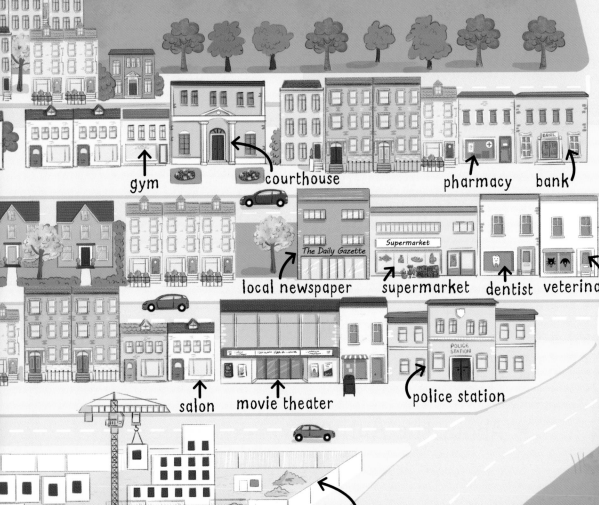

gym

courthouse

pharmacy

bank

The Daily Gazette

local newspaper

Supermarket

supermarket

dentist

veterinarian

salon

movie theater

POLICE STATION

police station

construction site

recycling center

fire station

hospital

restaurant

library

post office

café

school

Our school is right there. The other day, Theo
and I went to the school library to work on our
science project.

MEET MR. PAL

Mr. Pal is our school librarian. It is his job to help students find information in the library.

Hi! How can I help you today?

We need to do research for our science project.

We told Mr. Pal we were going to build a robotic jaw to show how sharks' teeth work. "We need to learn all about sharks!" I explained.

"I can help," Mr. Pal said. "Let's use the computer first to do an online search."

School librarians teach students how to be safe online. They help kids find trustworthy websites.

A call number is made up of numbers and letters. It tells what a book is about and where it should be on the library shelf.

Theo and I wanted to borrow some books about sharks, too. Mr. Pal helped us check the library catalog on the computer.

He told us nonfiction books have a call number and are arranged in order by subject.

There was a graphic novel near the shark books. "Whoops!" Mr. Pal said. "That book is in the wrong place. I'll move it. It's important to keep each book in the right spot so kids can find it."

We wanted to look for a nonfiction book about robotics. But those books were all checked out. Mr. Pal told us to try the public library.

Come back soon!

Fiction books are stories that are made up by an author. Nonfiction books give readers information about real things. Some books mix fiction and nonfiction.

Then Mr. Pal showed us how to check out using the scanner. That was fun!

AT THE PUBLIC LIBRARY

After school, Theo and I walked to the public library. The bookmobile was parked outside. A librarian was filling it with books.

A bookmobile is a library on wheels. People who can't get to the library can borrow books from the traveling bookmobile.

TODAY AT THE LIBRARY

We are open from **11 am to 8 pm.**

11 AM: Stories & Songs in the Children's Room

2 AM: English Language Class in Meeting Room 1

3 PM: Middle Grade Book Club in the Café

6 PM: Family Movie Night in the Lounge

1–6 PM: Maker Lab Open!

Look, a movie night!

That sounds fun!

Theo and I went to the children's room. On our way there, I saw my neighbor Carly. She works at the library after school. The library is a busy place. Carly told us about some of the places we might want to visit.

Circulation desk: People check out and return books at the circulation desk. It is usually near the front door.

Café: Many public libraries offer a café, where visitors can get something to eat or drink while reading library books.

Thanks for all the info!

So what are you going to do now?

Computer lab: Some people come here to use the library's computers. Users can do homework, go online, and even play games.

I'm going to reshelve these books.

Meeting rooms: Many libraries have meeting rooms where free classes in a new language, crafts, or other activities are held. People can also reserve meeting rooms for themselves.

MEET MS. McMAHON

Theo and I went to talk to the children's librarian. Her name was Ms. McMahon. I told her we were making a robotic shark jaw for a school project.

Welcome to your Library! YOU belong here!

We're looking for a book to help us make the robot.

I can help!

MS. McMAHON

Read More Books!

Children's librarians have a lot of jobs! They run book clubs and summer reading programs. They offer help with homework. The librarians also decide which books to buy for the library.

Ms. McMahon showed us the craft and how-to books. We found a book about building robots. Then she led us to the story time corner. "Every month we highlight books on a different subject," she said. "This month, many of our books about ocean life are here."

My mom and little sister come to story time every Saturday.

Many libraries have play spaces for kids. Some even have programs where kids can read to dogs!

Shells

Library Favorites

fish

ULTIMATE SHARKS

Octopus

How to Grow

Horses

STARS

THE JUNGLE

ELEPHANTS

THE OCEAN

WILD FLOWERS

All about OWLS

Animal Adventures

BIG CATS

Ms. McMahon asked us for our library cards. Then she used her scanner to check out our books.

A library card is free. It lets cardholders borrow books, movies, music, games, and magazines. Some libraries also loan out free passes to local museums.

Welcome to your Library! YOU belon here!

Book Return

"Have you been to our maker lab?" Ms. McMahon asked. "We have tools there that can help you build your robot."

Cool! I've always wanted to visit the lab.

MORE SHARKS!

MS. MCMAHON

"The maker lab has computers for creating video
games, lots of different building materials, and
a 3-D printer," Ms. McMahon told us.

Some public libraries loan out more than just books! People may be able to borrow baking pans, musical instruments, electronics, gardening tools, and even sports equipment.

A volunteer told us we could borrow supplies from the library. He helped Theo and me design and build our robotic shark jaw.

Theo and I had so much fun making our robot at the library.

We presented our project the next week. It was a big success!

A great white shark can go through 20,000 teeth in its life!

Ask a Librarian

Emma interviewed Ms. McMahon
for the school newspaper.

How many years did you study
to become a librarian?

Six years. I went to college for four
years. Then I continued my schooling
for two more years. I earned a master's
degree in library science.

Why did you become a librarian?

I love books, and I wanted to teach
and encourage others to read.

Why is reading so important?

Stories help you discover your own voice and find out more about who you are. They let you step into the shoes of people who have different lives and live in different places. Once you can read, you can learn about anything!

What is your favorite part of the job?

I enjoy working with kids and helping them find the information they need. And I love helping a reader discover a "just right" book for them!

Do you work on the weekends?

Sometimes! Public libraries are open nights and weekends. I may also attend bookfairs on weekends.

Ms. McMahon's Tips for Making the Most of Your Library

- The library is there for you. You are welcome anytime.

- Ask librarians anything! They are happy to help you find what you need.

- Take care of the library books and other materials you borrow and use.

- Return books and other materials on time. Someone else may be waiting.

- If you find a book you like, tell a friend about it!

A Librarian's Tools

Book return: Library staff collect books from this box and reshelve them.

Computer: Librarians can use this electronic machine to store, process, and retrieve large amounts of information.

Library card: This card helps librarians keep track of who borrowed which books and when they are due back.

Scanner: Librarians use this machine to check out someone's books.

Index

About the Author

AnnMarie Anderson has written numerous books for young readers–from easy readers to novels. She lives in Brooklyn, New York, with her husband and two sons. She visits the library as often as she can!